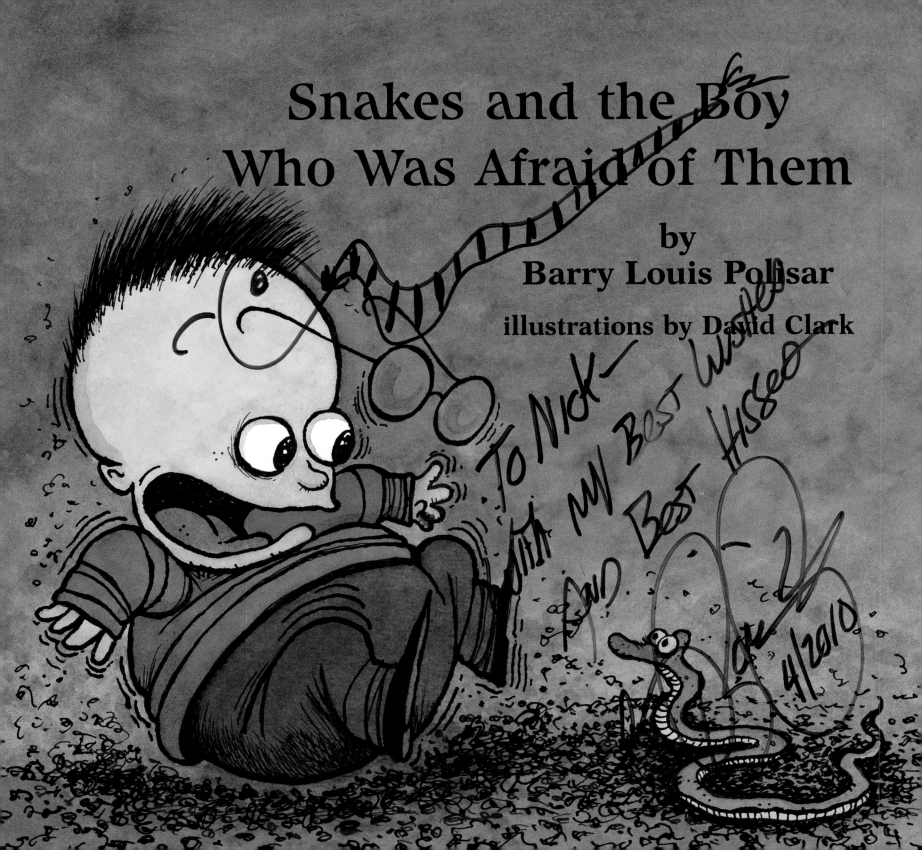

Snakes and the Boy
Who Was Afraid of Them

by
Barry Louis Polisar

illustrations by **David Clark**

Lenny was a normal boy. He liked to watch TV, ride his bike, and read books.

But there was something about Lenny that some people thought wasn't right. He was absolutely, positively, afraid of snakes.

When one of the girls at school brought in a baby black snake for "show-and-tell," Lenny panicked. He climbed on top of his desk and screamed, "Get me out of here!!!"

The other kids in his class laughed and after that they would tease him all the time.

Lisa and Edward, two kids who were always mean to everyone, were especially cruel.

They would come up to him on the playground, shout, "Snake!" and push him down.

He tried to pretend that he wasn't afraid of snakes but
everyone knew he really was.
And he was.

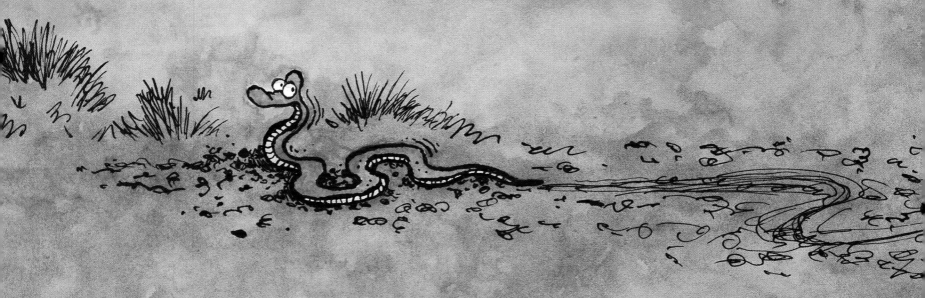

His teacher sent him to talk to the guidance counselor,
but it didn't help.

Then one day something terrible happened. Lenny arrived
at school to find that the class was going on a field trip.

They were going to the city zoo and one of the places they
were going to visit was the snake house.

That's the place where they keep all the snakes.

Lenny didn't want to go on the field trip, but everybody thought it would be good for him, so they made him go.

Lenny had always enjoyed the zoo, but today he hated it. All he could think about was going to the snake house.

When the class finally got there, they were met at the door by the zoo keeper. She explained what the children could expect to find inside. She told the children that some of the snakes were poisonous and that others were quite harmless. She said she would be taking some of the snakes out of their cases for the children to touch and to hold.

Everyone looked at Lenny. He announced that he was not going to go inside.

His teacher said, "Lenny, if you don't go in, you will be
in *big trouble*."
What could he do?

He went in.

The snake house was dark except for the lights coming from the glass cases. Everywhere Lenny looked he could see something wriggling behind the glass. He felt that eyes were staring out at him from every corner.

The zoo keeper removed a boa constrictor from its case and carefully passed it to the children to hold. Lisa and Edward pushed to the front to have their turn.

The boa was a very big snake. The zoo keeper said there was nothing to be afraid of, but Lenny would not go near it.

Lenny felt like they'd never leave the snake house, but finally, it was time to meet the school bus. The teacher thanked the zoo keeper and once everyone was outside she began to count the children. . . . "Twenty-one, twenty-two, twenty-three."

Two children were missing! Where did Lisa and Edward go?

No one knew.

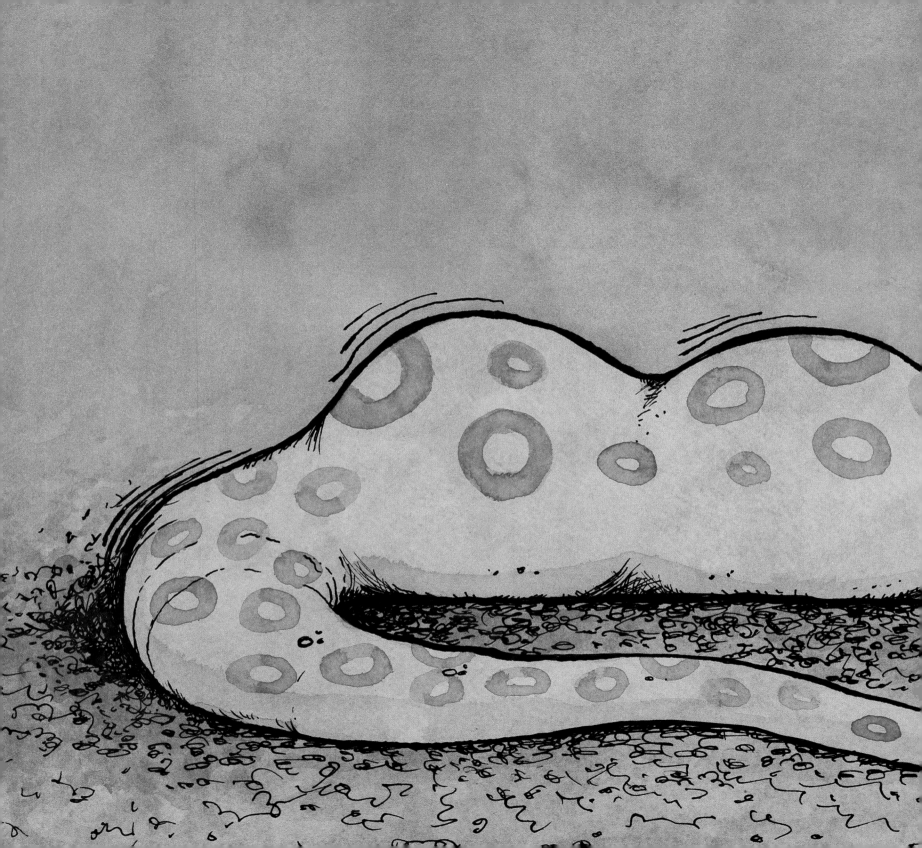

And they never found them either.

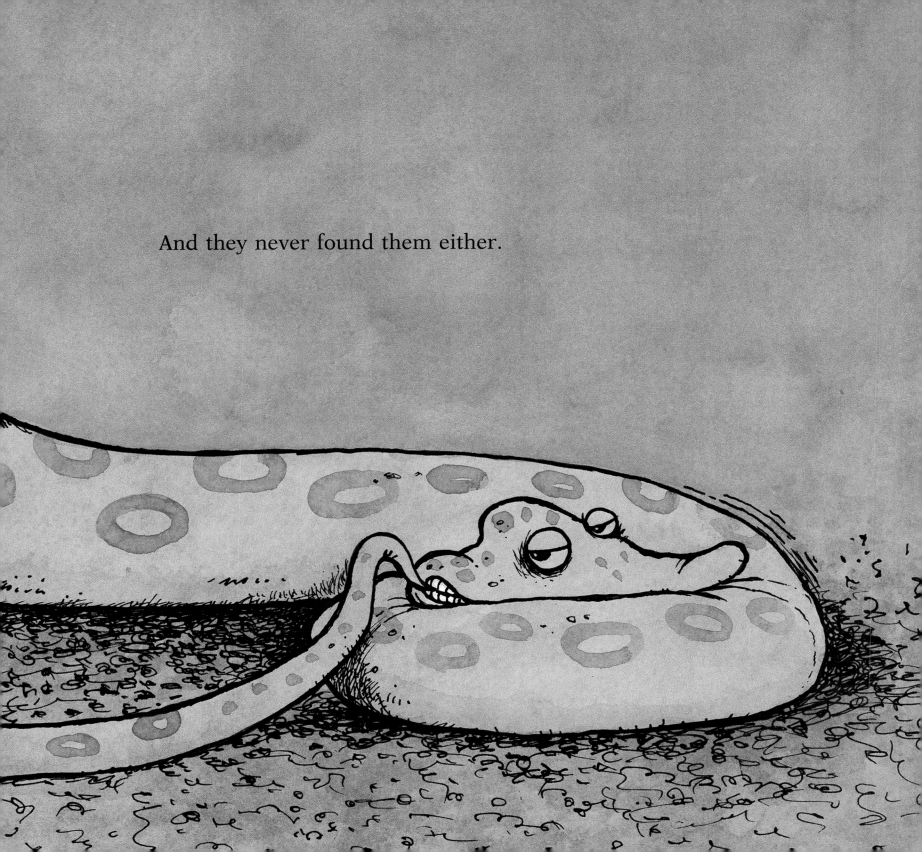

Lenny is still afraid of snakes.

Thanks again to Cousin Shelby
and my wife, Roni

Snakes and the Boy Who Was Afraid of Them
© 1987, 1988, 1993 by Barry Louis Polisar
Artwork © 1993 by David Clark

Published by Rainbow Morning Music
2121 Fairland Road; Silver Spring, MD 20904

Hardback ISBN 0-938663-15-1

This book was previously published in 1988
in a slightly different limited edition.